Roman Milisic & A. Richard Allen

APES-A-GO-GO!

HarperCollins *Children's Books*

Once upon a time there was a lovely town. It was so well kept that it was set to win the Tidiest Town Competition for the third year in a row.

Everything in it was perfect...

Everything, except for one flower, which had grown a little taller than the rest.

"Bah! That pesky flower," grumbled the town's pernickety mayor.

"Why, all it needs is a little nudge," said Fussy Great Ape,
who liked things just so. "I can fix it, Mr Mayor!"

And, delicately,
he did!

Unfortunately, he trampled the entire flower bed in the process!

"See what you've done, you Fussy Great Ape!" cried the irate mayor.

"Oops!" winced Fussy Great Ape.
"But, not to worry – I know just who can fix this."
And before the mayor could say a word, Fussy Great Ape lifted his head, pounded his chest, and yodeled,

(which is how Great Apes call each other).

Minutes later, who should turn up but **Mucky Great Ape**. A brilliant gardener, he took one look at the flower bed and said, "I can fix it, Mr Mayor!"

Yes, he replanted the flower bed...
Unfortunately, he muddied up the whole street in the process!

"GAH! Look at what you've done, you Mucky Great Ape!" barked the mayor from under a mountain of dirt.

"Oh, no!" cried the sorry ape. "But I know who can clean this up in a jiffy!"

So now both Great Apes threw back their shoulders, pounded their chests and hollered,

summoning...

Sopping Great Ape, who positively *loved* cleaning. He took one look at the muddy rumpus and said, "I can fix it, Mr Mayor!"

And, splish, splosh, he did...

...causing a huge
flood in the process.

"Why, you Sopping
Great Ape!" roared the
furious mayor, water
pouring from his pockets.

"Yikes!" said Sopping Great
Ape. "But worry not!"

Up went the apes' cry again,

"CUPPA COCOA! APES-a-GO-GO!"

And along came...
Thumping Great Ape.

"What you need is some drain holes," he said.

"I can fix that, Mr Mayor!"

And he did!

Kind of.

"Oh, you Thumping Great Ape!" wailed the mayor. "My beautiful town, it looks like Swiss cheese!"

"No good?" asked the hairy fellow, who had, after all, drained off all the water.

In no time at all, the apes were pounding their chests again, and raising the cry,

"CUPPA! COCOA! APES-A-GO-GO!"

to summon...

Sweeping Great Ape, who knew *exactly* how to get rid of holes.

Swishing and brushing, he got
rid of the holes, all right...

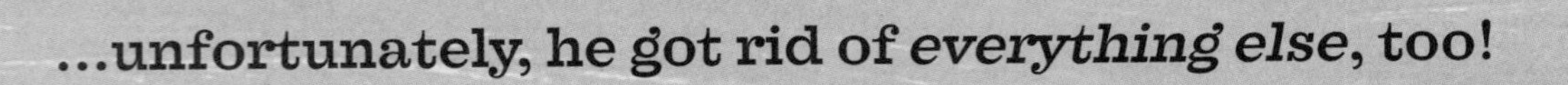

...unfortunately, he got rid of *everything else*, too!

"ARGHHH! You Sweeping Great Ape!"
frothed the enraged mayor. "My town! Ruined!"
Which was as much as you could get from him, as he
was now rolling on the ground, gnashing his teeth.

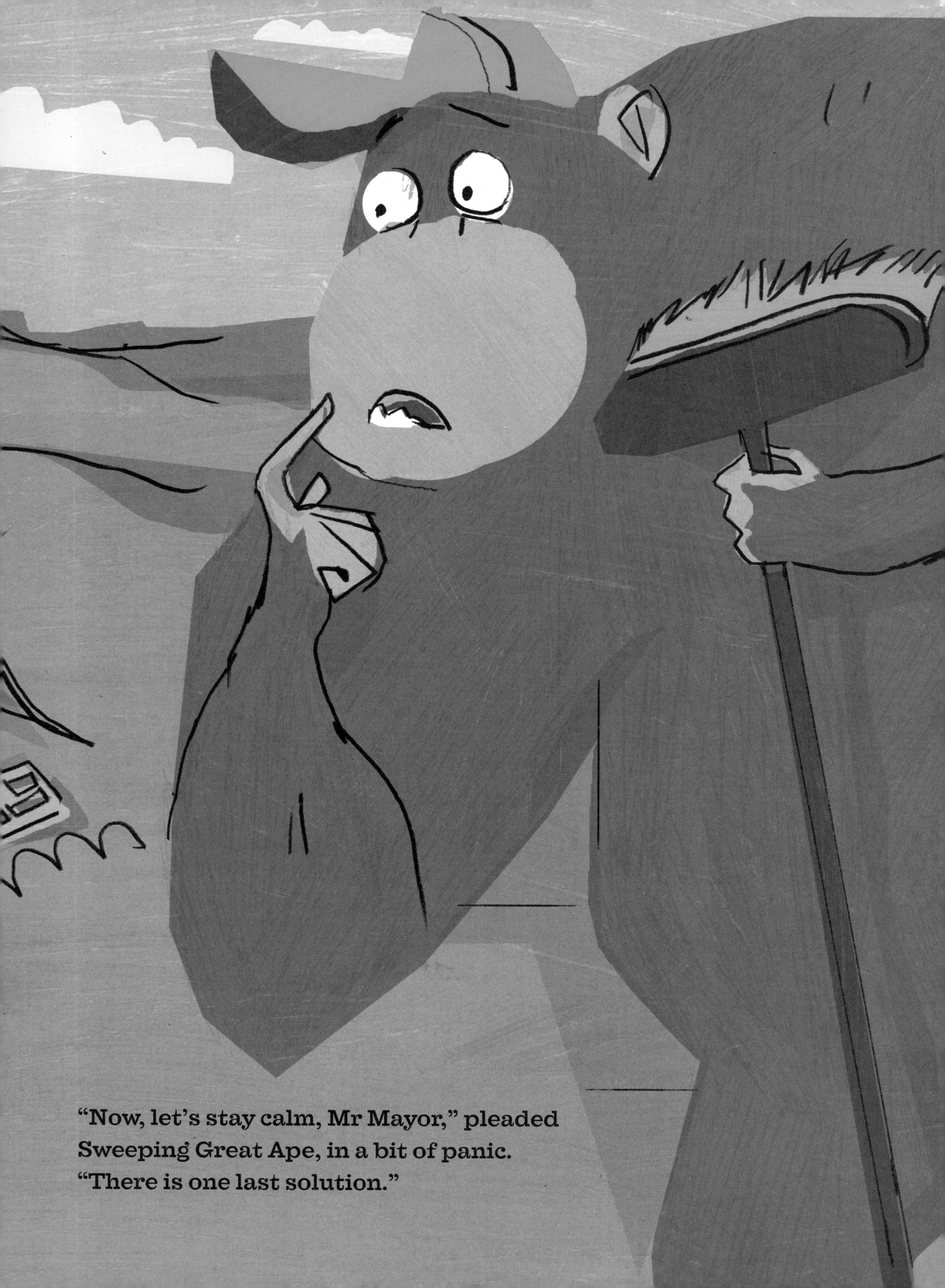

“Now, let’s stay calm, Mr Mayor,” pleaded Sweeping Great Ape, in a bit of panic. “There is one last solution.”

And together, all the Great Apes lifted their heads, pounded their chests and called at the tops of their voices,

"CUPPA! COCOA!

Apes-a-GO-GO!"

And who should turn up,
but **Baking Great Ape**.

“Well now, dears, I’m sure I can fix this!” smiled Baking Great Ape, for she had some experience in fixing disasters.

Then she baked a huge cake and put a little piece in front of the mayor who, through his tears, took a nibble.

"Mmm."

And then a little more.

"Yum."

All the townsfolk and all the Great Apes had a slice, too. Someone brought balloons. And, you know, people really started to enjoy themselves.

Meanwhile, the Great Apes were doing a fine job of putting things back together; maybe not quite as perfectly as before, but with plenty of charm.

At that moment, the mayor realised that maybe there was more to life than a perfect town. Like warm cake and good friends. He may not have the Tidiest Town any longer, but it just might be the *happiest*.

"Well, that was delicious," said the mayor, as he polished off the final crumb and folded his napkin neatly. "But who's going to clean up all these plates?"

"Allow me, Mr Mayor!" said **Smashing Great Ape**, who was near at hand.

The mayor thought about it for a moment...

"On second thoughts," he said,
"I think I'll do it myself."

And he did.